ISBN: 1492288500
ISBN 13: 9781492288503

Library of Congress Control Number: 2013915927
CreateSpace Independent Publishing Platform, North Charleston, SC

To my father and mother
Nancy
Suzie
Billy

This is the story of
Claire
who loves her hair
here, there and
everywhere.

Claire is sitting on her favorite stair
with not a lot of room to spare.
Just enough room for her beautiful hair.
Suddenly, out of nowhere
Claire happily declares,
"I think it's time to do my hair!"
Time to visit the extremely rare
Ms. Blare Sinclair.
She is the best anywhere.
She does Boom-Shaka-Laka hair!

Ms. Blare Sinclair does hair
in the town square
at Salon Hair Glare.
Many people are unaware that
Ms. Blare Sinclaire is super rare.
She does hair
with an amazing flair.
She does hair by a swivel chair.
She does hair beyond compare,
and the cost is more than fair.
Why go elsewhere?

Claire hurries to the center of
town square
to show off her beautiful hair.
Much to her surprise,
<u>no one is there!</u>
Oh well.
Good time for a delicious
chocolate eclaire
at Ms. Bea Fare's.

Claire buys a yummy
chocolate eclaire
from Ms. Bea Fare
to share
with her pig
Pierre
on the way,
to the fair,
in the wide open air.

Claire is flying in midair
with her pig Pierre.
What a pair!
<u>Claire and Pierre!</u>
Off they go
to the fair.

When Claire and Pierre
arrive at the fair
there is
excitement everywhere.
Elephants! Cows!
<u>Look!</u>
Over there.
The bear is in the air.

Tickets

Claire's veterinarian,
Dr. Kitty McNare,
is very very aware.
She can heal and repair
boo boos anywhere.
Dr. Kitty McNare
treats all her patients with
tender, loving care.

It may not seem fair.
Claire has wash and wear hair.
It takes very little care,
which gives her time to spare,
with her many friends
at the fancy affair.

Claire shows up at the fancy affair.
She's all dressed up,
and has beautiful hair.
Extraordinaire!
She feels like a millionaire!
Tons of fun to share,
with her friends from here,
there and everywhere.

Claire without a care.
She's dreaming of
dancing in the air.

Time to stop and mend a tear
that came from out of nowhere.
With careful care,
Claire will repair the tear.
Then to the kitchen
to see baby sister
Cher.

Claire's
Cart

Claire's baby sister Cher,
with <u>her</u> beautiful hair,
waits in the high chair
for the dinner
Claire will prepare.

COOKIES

GUM

SUGAR

Jam Jelly Juice

At the end of the day,
Claire is in her comfy chair,
with her favorite books everywhere.
Claire says,
"I love to read, I swear.
Don't take my books.
Don't you dare!"

Claire had a nightmare
full of despair.
She had a dream
her hair was not there.
It gave her quite a scare.

When she awoke,
she threw her arms in the air.
All of her beautiful hair
was still there!

Claire rides her mare
Scarlett O'hare,
that she won at the fair,
to receive an award,
from the mayor
of town square,
for the most beautiful hair.
Here, there and everywhere.

Made in the USA
Lexington, KY
16 February 2014